Welcome to The Giggle Club

The Giggle Club is a collection of new picture books made to put a giggle into early reading. There are funny stories about a contrary mouse, a dancing fox, a turtle with a trumpet, a pig with a ball, a hungry monster, a laughing lobster, an elephant who sneezes away the jungle and lots more! Each of these characters is a member of **The Giggle Club**, but anyone can join: just pick up a **Giggle Club** book, read it and get giggling!

Turn to the checklist on the inside back cover and tick off the **Giggle Club** books you have read.

TEE HEE!

HA HA!

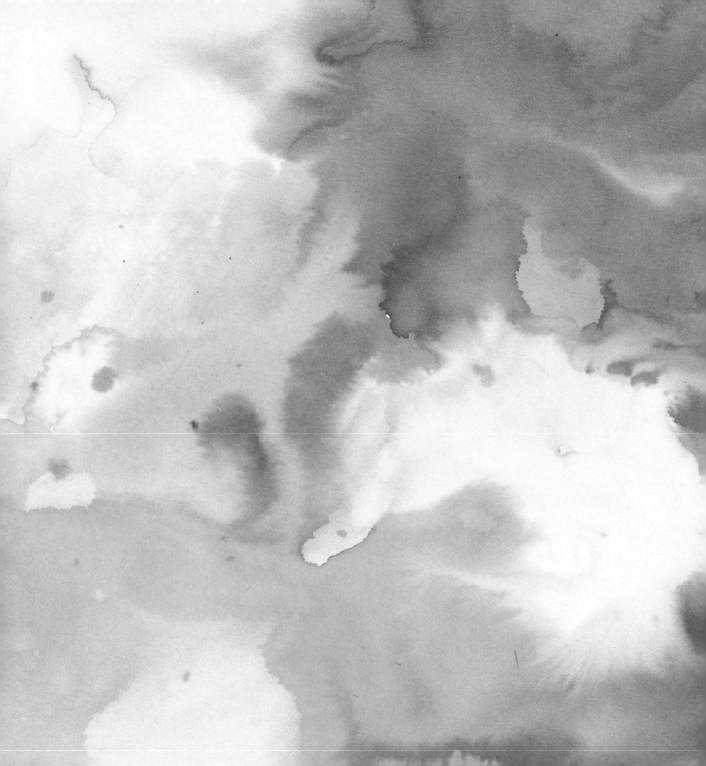

For Lucy

First published 1996 by Walker Books Ltd
87 Vauxhall Walk, London SE11 5HJ

This edition published 1997

10 9 8 7 6 5 4 3

© 1996 Colin West

This book has been typeset in Plantin.

Printed in Hong Kong

British Library Cataloguing in Publication Data
A catalogue record for this book
is available from the British Library.

ISBN 0-7445-5463-2

Buzz, Buzz, Buzz, went Bumblebee

Colin West

WALKER BOOKS
AND SUBSIDIARIES
LONDON · BOSTON · SYDNEY

Buzz, buzz, buzz, went Bumble-bee.

.....as he landed on Rabbit's ear.....

Rabbit said,
"Buzz off!"

...Buzz, buzz, buzz, went Bumble-bee...

...Buzz, buzz, buzz, went Bumble-bee....

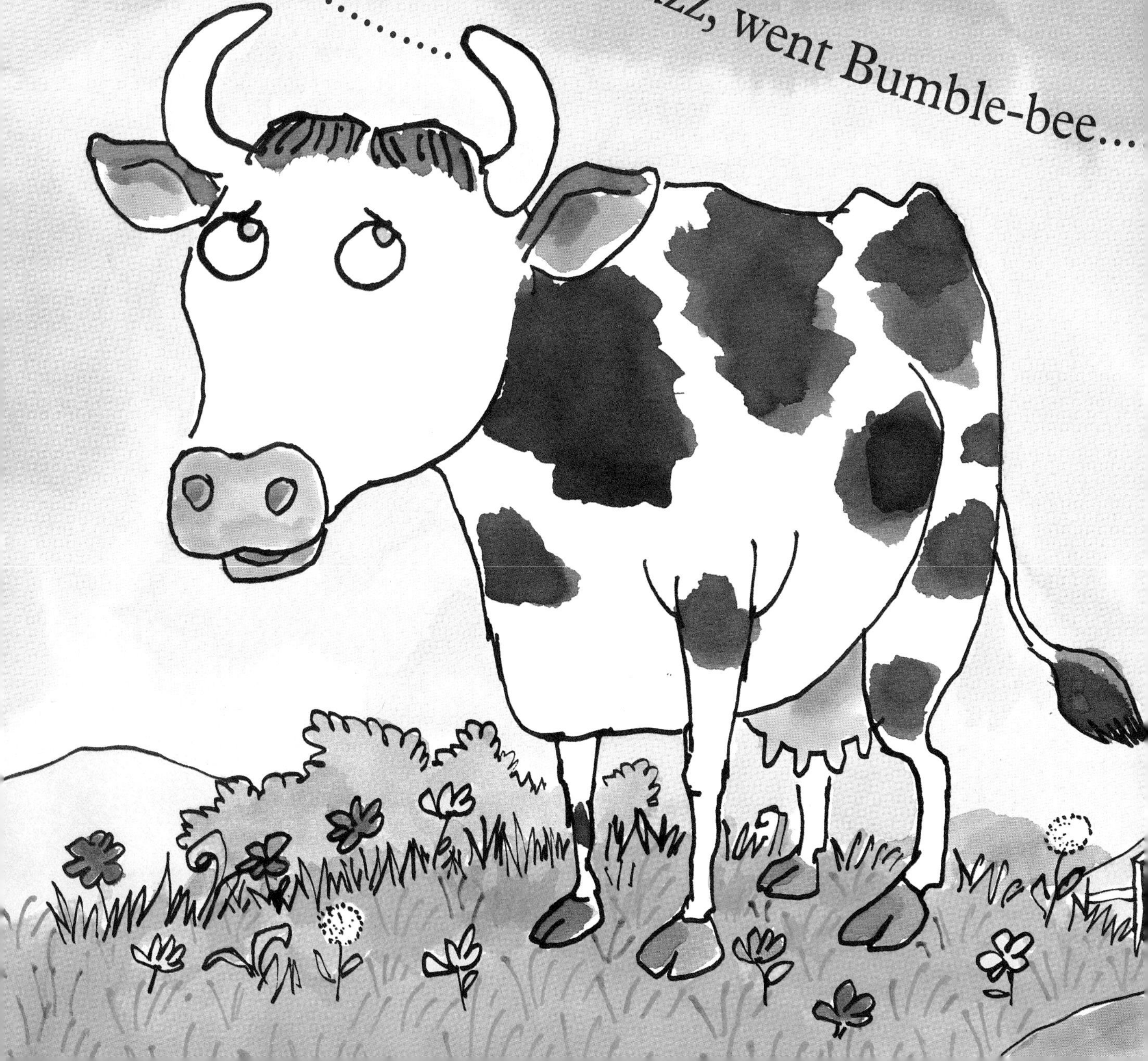

...as he landed on Crow's beak...

Crow said, "Buzz off!"

...Buzz, buzz, buzz, went Bumble-bee...........

...Buzz, buzz, buzz, went Bumble-bee...........

.........as he landed on Butterfly's wing.........

Butterfly
said:

..........together.

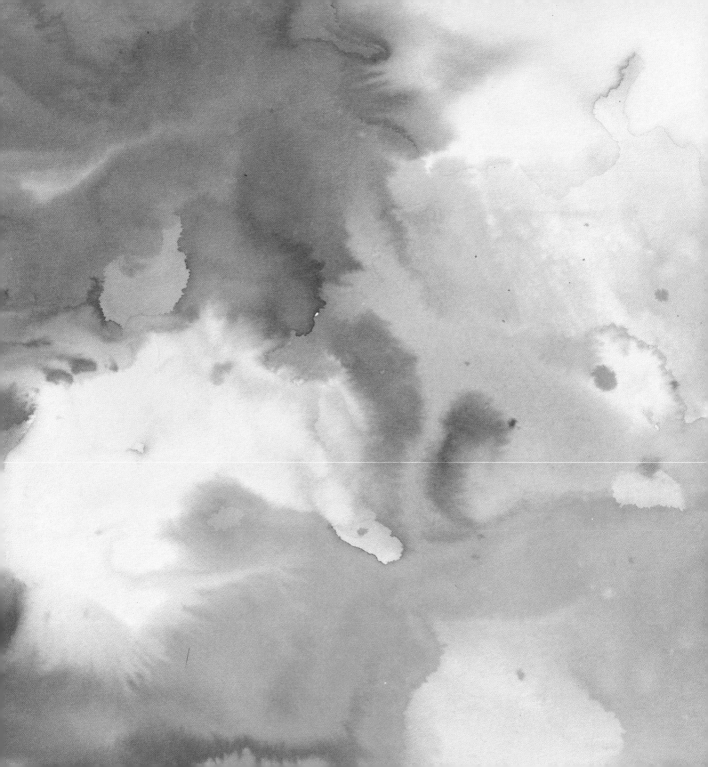